FAIRYTALE NINJAS

Two and a Half Wishes

T0371283

Books by Paula Harrison

FAIRYTALE NINJAS

Two and a Half Wishes

PAULA HARRISON

Illustrated by Mónica de Rivas

HarperCollins *Children's Books*

First published in the United Kingdom by
HarperCollins *Children's Books* in 2024
HarperCollins *Children's Books* is a division of HarperCollins*Publishers* Ltd
1 London Bridge Street
London SE1 9GF

www.harpercollins.co.uk

HarperCollins*Publishers*
Macken House, 39/40 Mayor Street Upper
Dublin 1, D01 C9W8, Ireland

1

ISBN 978–0–00–858301–9

Paula Harrison and Mónica de Rivas assert the moral right to be
identified as the author and illustrator of the work respectively.

A CIP catalogue record for this title is available from the British Library.

Typeset in New Century Schoolbook
Printed and bound in the UK using 100% renewable electricity
at CPI Group (UK) Ltd

This book contains FSC™ certified paper and other controlled
sources to ensure responsible forest management.

For more information visit: www.harpercollins.co.uk/green

For Maureen

WAYBEYOND

SNOWFELL PEAKS

RIPPLING RIVER

HOLLOW MOUNTAIN

SHIMMERING LAKE

WATERBURY

MURKWEED LAKE

DIAMOND PALACE

SCORCH ISLAND

RIPPLING RIVER

GOLDEN VALLEY

BIG HOLLOW
TREE LIBRARY

SHADOWMOON
FOREST

MIRROR FALLS

RUMPELSTILTSKIN'S
HOUSE

HOBBLETON

GRIMSTONE CASTLE

REDROCK CANYON

CHAPTER ONE

'Try this, Caramel! Do you like it?' Goldie Locks gave a spoonful of porridge to her little bear cub.

Caramel licked the spoon and squeaked eagerly. Standing up on her back legs, she put her front paws on Goldie's knee and gazed at her with wide brown eyes.

Goldie smiled and gave the bear cub another

spoonful. Then she stirred the porridge one more time before putting the lid on the huge copper saucepan. 'That's done! Now let's get out of here while we still have the chance!'

Grabbing a basket, she popped Caramel inside along with some squares of flapjack and a bag of cherries. Then she sneaked out of the back door of the Three Spoons Hotel and dashed across the market square.

Goldie breathed a sigh of relief as soon as she was round the corner. The hotel guests always loved her porridge, but she didn't want to spend all morning at the stove. She frowned as she wiped a blob of porridge off her sleeve. She hadn't told her mum and dad, but . . . she was really bored of porridge! Why couldn't the guests have something else for breakfast? She pulled a flapjack out of her basket and took a huge bite.

Heading down a side street, she found Red Riding and Snow White waiting for her at the edge of town. 'Sorry I'm late!' she called, running to meet them. 'I've only just finished cooking. Why aren't we meeting at the academy?'

'The whole place is full of beginners learning to tap-dance,' Red said gloomily.

Snow held up a bundle of ninja costumes. 'I brought our suits. Let's go somewhere quiet and practise our ninja moves.'

Red's eyes lit up. 'Shall we go to Shadowmoon Forest? We could try out the Creeping Tree and Shadow Flit moves that Madame Hart taught us last week. I bet I can be quieter and sneakier than either of you!'

Goldie grinned. 'I bet you can't! You're the noisiest girl I know! Snow's always the best at ninja moves.'

Snow, who had stopped to stroke a wild rabbit, smiled and passed the ninja suits to her friends.

Goldie, Red and Snow lived in Hobbleton, a sleepy little town in the magical Kingdom of Waybeyond. Red delivered baskets of food for her

mum who ran the Pickled Pantry grocery store, while Snow helped out in her family's dress shop. The three girls were really good friends and took ballet lessons together at the Glass Slipper Academy. Their adventures had begun when they'd discovered that their teacher, Madame Hart, had a secret storeroom full of swords, shields and other equipment that she'd collected while training young sword-fighters many years ago. This secret stash was hidden behind a mirrored wall in the main dance studio and, once they'd discovered it all, Goldie, Red and Snow had wanted to give up ballet lessons at once and learn sword-fighting and ninja moves instead.

After a lot of persuading, Madame Hart had agreed to train them. Since then, they'd used their

new skills to fight trolls, ride dragons and defeat some of the wickedest baddies the kingdom had ever seen! Goldie knew there was more to learn, and she couldn't wait! It would be MUCH more exciting than cooking porridge.

'Hurry up then, slowcoaches!' she called over her shoulder. 'The first one to the woods gets the biggest piece of my flapjack!'

Goldie, Red and Snow dashed out of Hobbleton and across the fields to Shadowmoon Forest. A herd of unicorns wandered through the trees. The girls raced down the twisty woodland track past a row of giant red toadstools. Tinkling laughter echoed through the leaves as a cluster of fairies whizzed by.

Stopping in a clearing, Goldie, Red and Snow shared out some of the flapjacks before wriggling into their ninja suits. Goldie admired how much her outfit blended in with the branches and leaves – the perfect camouflage! Caramel scrambled out of her basket and began climbing up a tree.

'The Creeping Tree move went like this . . .' Red tiptoed from one tree trunk to the next.

'And the Shadow Flit was like this!' Snow sprang from one shadowy spot to another.

Goldie shook her head. 'You're not doing it right! Red, you have to crouch much lower than that, and, Snow, don't stick your arms out so much.'

'Let's see you do it – if you're so perfect!' said Red, sticking her hands on her hips.

'Easy! Watch this!' Goldie smoothed the wrinkles out of her ninja costume and got into position behind a tree. Then she crept through the wood like a shadow. She was just about to try the next move when she spotted someone in a grey cloak moving between the trees. The cloaked figure had their hood pulled up so Goldie couldn't see their face, but something about them seemed familiar.

'Who's that?' murmured Snow.

Goldie looked closer. 'I think it might be one of our new hotel guests – Miss Raven. She only arrived yesterday.'

'Doesn't she realise this forest is full of magical creatures?' Red said, frowning. 'We're used to them, but if she runs into a troll or gets stuck in the middle of a unicorn stampede she could get seriously hurt!'

'Maybe we should warn her,' said Snow.

Goldie peered through the trees. Miss Raven had stopped beside a giant toadstool and was taking a large jam jar out of her pocket when suddenly a distant rumbling growl echoed round the wood.

'Troll!' cried Red. 'And it sounds like it's heading this way. We'd better tell her!'

'Wait!' hissed Snow. 'We can't let anyone see us dressed like this.'

Quickly pulling their normal clothes over their ninja suits, the girls raced over to Miss Raven with Caramel scampering after them.

'Miss Raven!' Goldie called out. 'There's a troll close by! You should probably get back to Hobbleton.'

Miss Raven swung round, her eyes narrowing when she saw the three girls. She was a tall woman with dark eyes, and her grey cloak shimmered as she moved. 'Goodness, you made me jump!' she said, frowning. 'It's Goldie, isn't it? What are you doing out here in the woods?'

'Um . . . just going for a walk,' Goldie said quickly. 'But then we heard a troll so we thought we'd better warn you.' She glanced at Miss Raven's empty jam jar and wondered what it was for.

Miss Raven tucked the jar under her cloak. 'Well, I was just looking for some woodland flowers, but I certainly don't want to meet any trolls. They sound terrifying!' She smiled thinly. 'I'll see you back at the hotel then, Goldie. Be careful, girls. You could meet all sorts of crooks and baddies in a forest like this!' She marched away with her cloak billowing out behind her.

'Huh!' snapped Red. 'We're not afraid of ANYTHING in this forest. We even fought a troll here once!'

'Shh! She'll hear you!'

whispered Snow. 'No one's meant to know – remember?'

Goldie watched Miss Raven disappear through the trees. 'That was weird . . .' she said slowly.

'What do you mean?' asked Snow.

'She didn't seem that worried about the troll, did she? And what was she doing with that jam jar?' said Goldie.

Red shrugged. 'She was picking flowers. She probably brought the jar to put them in. Come on, we'd better head back.'

Goldie lifted Caramel into her basket and followed the others. Thoughts whirled through her head. There was something odd about Miss Raven with her sharp eyes and long shimmering cloak. If only she could work out what it was.

CHAPTER TWO

When Goldie slipped through the back door of the hotel a while later, the kitchen was still filled with the smell of porridge. Her dad was there, loading bags of potatoes and turnips into the pantry. He took off his checked cap and rubbed his forehead.

'There you are, Goldie!' he said, beaming. 'The guests loved your porridge this morning.'

'Thanks, Dad!' Goldie set down her basket

and Caramel clambered out.

Mr Locks poured two cups of tea and offered Goldie the last slice of cherry cake.

'It's okay, Dad!' said Goldie, smiling. 'I know it's your favourite.'

Her dad smiled back. 'If you're heading upstairs, could you take some towels to room five? Your mum went out to the bakery, and I've been rushed off my feet all morning.'

'Don't worry – I'll do it right now!'

Goldie hurried upstairs and took some towels out of the laundry cupboard. Knocking on the guest-room door, she suddenly remembered that this was Miss Raven's room. When no one answered, she opened the door and slipped inside.

The curtains were drawn, and a bedside lamp cast a pale light over the room. A row of glass bottles filled with blue, green and purple liquids

 23

stood on the chest of drawers. A book with a black leather cover lay beside them. Leaving the towels on the bed, Goldie crept closer to read the title: *How to Make Your Spells Sparkle*.

Spells! Goldie caught her breath. Why did Miss Raven have a book about spells? Then everything began to slot together like a jigsaw puzzle. First there was Miss Raven's shimmering cloak, then the potion bottles and now this book! She must be an enchantress with magical powers.

Reaching out to open the book, Goldie stopped suddenly. What was that strange noise? It sounded like a trapped bee or a wasp buzzing against a window. Following the sound, Goldie opened one of the drawers . . . and discovered Miss Raven's jam jar with a frightened fairy flying around inside.

'You poor thing!' cried Goldie, picking up the jar.

The fairy whizzed round and round, bashing against the inside of the jar with her tiny fists.

Her glittering purple wings fluttered faster and faster, leaving fairy dust smudged all over the glass.

Goldie glanced at the door. If she opened the jar, Miss Raven would know someone had been in her room and looked through her things. The enchantress might even guess who'd done it. Did she really want to mess with a sorceress with a book full of magic spells? It could be even more dangerous than facing a troll or riding a dragon!

Goldie's heart thumped. She had to be brave. She couldn't leave that poor fairy trapped in there. Taking a deep breath, she gripped the lid of the jar and twisted it. The lid popped off, and the fairy burst out. Shaking her glittery wings, she hovered in front of Goldie's face.

'Thank you so much!' she cried, her eyes full of tears. 'I will never forget your great kindness and—'

The door creaked.

The fairy froze, her eyes wide. Then she zipped away from Goldie and hid behind the red checked curtains. Goldie spun round, her heart sinking.

Miss Raven was standing in the doorway, her eyes flashing like lightning. 'How DARE you come in here and mess with my things!' she hissed, marching towards Goldie.

Goldie swallowed. 'That's what you were doing in the woods this morning. You were trying to trap a fairy, weren't you? Well, you shouldn't have done it – it's really mean!'

'You have no idea how much trouble you're

in!' Miss Raven snarled, grabbing the empty jar from Goldie's hands.

Goldie stumbled backwards and bumped into the chest of drawers, knocking the potion bottles over.

'Is something wrong here?' Goldie's dad appeared in the doorway. 'Goldie, are you all right?'

Miss Raven swung round. 'This GIRL came into my room and—'

'That's my fault!' Mr Locks smiled gently. 'I asked Goldie to bring you some clean towels. I'm sorry if she disturbed you. Our guests' comfort is very important to us. Is there anything else you need?'

'I will NOT put up with this!' Miss Raven snatched up the spellbook. Flicking to a page in the middle, she began chanting loudly:

 27

'Take this spell and make it roll!

Turn this man into a troll . . .'

'Dad, I think we'd better go!' Goldie tugged frantically at her dad's arm.

A tiny spark leaped from Miss Raven's little finger and scorched the bedclothes.

'Now hold on a minute!' began Mr Locks, but Miss Raven was still chanting.

'Take this spell and— Frogspawn! Where's my troll spell?' The enchantress lost her place and began flicking through the book again. Suddenly green sparks flew out of her fingertips and struck Mr Locks in the chest.

'Dad!' yelled Goldie. 'Are you all right?'

'I'm not really sure . . . Maybe I'll sit down,' gulped Mr Locks, sinking on to the bed.

Little by little, he began to shrink. Feathers sprouted on his arms, and his nose grew long

and beaklike. Finally, he stretched out a pair of
feathery grey wings and waddled across the bed
with a loud quack!

Goldie stared in shock. Where her dad had been just a second before stood a large mallard duck with a green head and a yellow beak.

Miss Raven slammed the book shut, muttering to herself. 'Vole vomit! That's not a troll! Why aren't these spells working?'

Goldie knelt down by the duck. 'Dad, are you all right? Can you hear me?'

'See what happens when you get in my way? You should have kept your nose out of my business!' snapped Miss Raven.

'Dad! Don't worry, I'll help you.' Goldie tried to scoop the duck up in her arms, but he quacked noisily, shaking his beak. Then he fluttered out of the door and waddled away along the corridor.

Goldie turned back to Miss Raven, tears pricking her eyes. 'You can't leave him like that! Turn him back!'

Miss Raven fixed Goldie with an icy glare. 'If you want your father back to normal, you'd better do EXACTLY as I say. Bring me three fairies by sunset tomorrow, or your dad will stay like that forever!' And she pushed Goldie out of the room and shut the door in her face.

Goldie stared after the duck, who was still waddling away down the passage. Catching fairies and handing them over to an evil enchantress would be a horrible thing to do. But she couldn't let her poor dad be a duck forever. She had to find Red and Snow at once! They would help her work out how to defeat Miss Raven and get her dad back again.

As she hurried down the corridor, something buzzed close to her ear. The fairy, who'd been hiding behind the curtain, zoomed past in a flurry of fairy dust. Then she zipped out of an open window and flew away into the cloudy grey sky.

CHAPTER THREE

Goldie rushed after her dad, hoping she could hide him somewhere before her mum saw. Then she would find a way to fix everything before anyone discovered what was wrong.

The duck flapped his wings and quacked noisily as Goldie chased after him. At last, she caught him, scooped him up under one arm and dived into an empty bathroom. Running a nice deep bath, she gently put the duck into the water. Then she fetched some seeds and berries and left them on the edge of the bath. Her dad quacked happily and swam around, dipping his beak into the water and fluffing his feathers.

Goldie sighed. At least he'd be happy there. 'I'll be back soon,' she told him. 'And I'll find a way to reverse that spell, I promise.'

Hurrying downstairs, she found Caramel under the kitchen table eating the last of the flapjacks. Gathering up the little bear cub, she ran straight to the Pickled Pantry to look for Red.

'Hello, Goldie! I'm afraid Red's gone out,' said Mrs Riding, busily tidying the shelves. 'She left a message for you and Snow to meet her at the Glass Slipper Academy. Something about a spare practice room.'

'Thank you!' Goldie rushed out of the shop.

Crossing the market square, she turned a corner. Then she ran along the next street and through the archway that led to the Glass Slipper Academy.

Piano music and the sound of tap-dancing drifted out of the window of the main studio. Goldie ran inside and quickly searched the other rooms. She found Red and Snow in a small room at the back, whirling around in front of a mirror as they practised their sword-fighting moves. Goldie set Caramel down on the floor and tried to get her breath back. The bear cub trundled over to the mirror and sat down.

'Oh good – you got my message,' began Red, but Goldie didn't wait for her to finish.

'Something terrible has happened!' she burst out, and in a rush she explained about the trapped fairy and how Miss Raven had turned her dad into a duck.

Snow went pale. 'Your poor dad! Did it hurt?'

'I don't think so,' said Goldie. 'He seemed quite happy swimming around in the bath when I left, but I have to find a way to turn him back again, and Miss Raven says she won't reverse the spell unless I bring her three fairies by sunset tomorrow.'

'Three fairies! What does she want them for?' asked Snow.

Goldie took a long gulping breath and blinked back some tears. 'I don't know! I'm just really worried about my dad.'

Snow put an arm round her. 'Don't worry! We're a team, and we'll sort this out together.'

'Miss Raven won't get away with this!' Red scowled. 'Let's get some swords from the storeroom and go and find her.'

'We can't just rush in, waving our swords,' said Snow. 'She could turn us all into ducks! We need to wait a bit and work out what she's up to.'

'I'd rather fight her first and ask questions later,' grumbled Red.

'Please don't do that!' a tinkly voice piped up. 'She's the meanest enchantress I've met in a long, long time.'

The girls spotted a fairy sitting on the curtain rail above the window. Her tiny legs dangled over the rail, and her purple wings were folded behind her back.

'You're the fairy that was trapped in the jar, aren't you?' said Goldie.

'Yes, I am! And I followed you here to thank you properly for setting me free.' The fairy fluttered down to hover beside Goldie. 'That nasty enchantress caught me this morning while

I was sunning myself on a wood lily. There I was – dreaming about moonlit parties and forest dancing – and WHOOSH! She clapped a jar over my head and took me away as if I was some sort of beetle that she wanted to collect.'

'That must have been awful!' said Snow.

'And my magic didn't work through the jam jar, so I could have been trapped forever if you hadn't let me out,' the fairy went on. 'You are MY HERO!' And she showered Goldie with glitter.

'Um, that's okay!' said Goldie, trying to brush the glitter out of her hair. 'I couldn't leave you stuck in there.'

'Well, I am SUPER GRATEFUL! So I've decided to grant you all some fairy wishes to help you defeat that evil enchantress. It's really the least I can do! Wishes always come in threes, of course, so you'll have three whole wishes to help you!' The fairy beamed.

'Ooh, wishes! They could really come in handy,' said Snow.

The fairy took a deep breath and lifted her hand high in the air. 'ONE!' she cried with a flick of her wand.

A sparkly purple flash filled the room, leaving spots dancing in front of the girls' eyes. Caramel gave a squeak of excitement and scampered over to cling on to Goldie's leg.

Red rubbed her eyes. 'Hey! You might have warned us before you—'

'TWO!' shrieked the fairy, flicking her wand again, and another purple flash dazzled the girls.

Glitter drifted gently to the floor. Caramel jumped up and down in delight. Then she accidentally breathed in some glitter and gave an enormous sneeze.

'Last one!' squealed the fairy, fluttering down a little. 'Are you ready? And THREE!' But, just as she waved her wand, Caramel bounced into the air, growling excitedly.

The bear cub grabbed the end of the fairy's wand in her teeth just before the wish popped out. SNAP! The tiny wand broke in half, and Caramel skipped round the room with a sparkly bit of wand poking out of her mouth.

'Caramel, that's really naughty! Give it back!' cried Goldie.

The fairy stared at the snapped wand in her hand. 'Oh dear! I'm afraid you only got half of the last wish. What a shame!'

'So we haven't got three wishes after all?' said Red. 'Can't you make us some more?'

'Not with a wand like this!' The fairy waved her broken stick. 'Now remember that your wishes are precious, so use them wisely. Also, you can't make a wish against the enchantress directly – she's too magical for that! So you won't be able to make her disappear or banish her to some faraway land.'

'What good are these wishes if we can't use them against Miss Raven?' asked Red.

'Oh, don't worry! I'm sure you'll think of something,' the fairy said brightly.

 41

Goldie finally caught Caramel and took the piece of broken wand away from her. The fairy swooped down to pick it up.

'I'd better head back to Shadowmoon Forest to mend this,' she told them. 'Good luck with your two and a half wishes.'

'Two and a half? Don't you mean two wishes?' asked Goldie. 'What are we supposed to do with half a wish?'

But the fairy had already whizzed out of the window and disappeared into the sky.

CHAPTER FOUR

'I know what to do with the first wish,' Goldie said firmly. 'I'm going to wish my dad back to normal right now.' She scooped up Caramel and headed for the door.

'Wait, Goldie!' cried Snow. 'I know you want your dad back, but I don't think you should do it straight away.'

'Why not?' demanded Goldie. 'I can't leave

him paddling round the bath all day.'

'Just think for a minute,' said Snow. 'If you use the first wish to undo that duck spell, then Miss Raven will know that we've got magical powers too. It'll make her suspicious, and we don't even know what she's up to yet. Did she tell you what she's doing here?'

Goldie rubbed her forehead. 'No, she didn't really explain.'

'That's why I think we should spy on her for a while and find out why she's in Hobbleton,' Snow went on. 'She won't spot us if we wear our ninja costumes, and we'll still have the fairy wishes to use when we're ready.'

'And we can take our swords with us,' added Red. 'Just in case!'

Goldie sighed. She didn't like the idea of leaving her dad as a duck, but Snow was right.

 44

They needed to discover what Miss Raven was doing and why she was capturing fairies.

'Okay, let's spy on her for a while,' she said. 'But, as soon as we work out what that nasty enchantress is up to, I'm using a wish to break the spell.'

There was a rush of voices and footsteps in the corridor outside.

'That must be the end of the tap-dancing lesson,' said Red. 'Once they've gone, we can fetch the swords and all the other things we need.'

Goldie, Red and Snow waited till all the younger children had streamed down the academy steps with their dance bags. Then they sneaked into the main studio and used the handle behind the famous glass slipper to open the secret door in the mirror. A hidden storeroom full of swords, shields and ninja costumes lay behind the door, and bright starlight poured from a magical crown hanging from the ceiling.

Goldie gazed at the shelves of equipment, wondering what to take. Caramel scampered in after her and began playing with the flying carpet snoozing in the corner.

'Here – have this!' Red grabbed a wooden training sword and handed another one to Goldie. 'Snow, do you want your bow and arrows?'

Goldie packed a few extra things into a rucksack – a candle, a raincoat and a roll of sticky tape – not really sure what she might need.

'I think that's everything except for food!' Red said, peering into her own rucksack. 'I did have some muffins in here, but then I ate them all. I WISH we had a proper picnic.'

There was a flash of bright purple light and a whoosh of air. Then a large picnic hamper appeared, piled high with cheese-and-pickle sandwiches, jam tarts, chocolate cake, bread rolls and heaps of pears, apples and oranges, along with a folded-up rug and some gleaming white plates.

The three girls stared at the hamper in shock.

'Oh no!' cried Snow. 'What have you done, Red?'

'You've used up one of our wishes!' stormed Goldie, her face reddening. 'How could you do that? Now we've only got one left.'

Red's shoulders slumped. 'I didn't mean to! It just sort of slipped out. I'm really sorry.'

'I needed that wish for my dad!' cried Goldie, stomping up and down.

Caramel whimpered and the flying carpet rolled itself up and hid behind a stack of shields at the back of the storeroom.

'I said I'm sorry!' said Red. 'I'd take it back if I could.'

'We still have one wish left – maybe more if the half a wish works somehow,' Snow said soothingly. 'We may as well take some of this food with us. We definitely can't carry the whole hamper.'

They each grabbed some sandwiches, cake and fruit and stuffed everything into their rucksacks. Caramel had already eaten one of the jam tarts.

'I can't believe we only have ONE wish left!' said Goldie as they headed out of the academy. 'From now on, nobody is allowed to say W-I-S-H.' She spelled the word out carefully. 'We absolutely cannot waste another one!'

Red and Snow exchanged looks, but for once Red stayed quiet.

Bright sunlight poured down as they made their way up the street with Caramel gambolling along behind them. Goldie felt her bad mood lifting. They still had one wish left after all, and that would be enough to undo the spell on her dad.

'The last time I saw Miss Raven she was in her room,' she explained to the others. 'I reckon we can climb up the ivy and peek through her window to see what she's doing.'

'We don't need to – look!' Red pointed to a

figure in a grey cloak crossing the market square.

Miss Raven swept past the ice dragon that was snoozing by a market stall – a creature that had arrived several weeks before after a huge magical mix-up. Then she stopped and swung round, as if she was checking to see who might be watching. The girls dodged behind a wooden cart to avoid being spotted.

Goldie picked up Caramel and stashed the little bear cub in her rucksack, leaving only

the cub's eyes, nose and ears poking out of the top. Then, together, the girls crept across the street. Goldie led the way, using her ninja training to stay out of sight. She did a Belly

Crawl move under the wooden cart, followed by a Silent Statue as Miss Raven stopped to look in the bakery window.

Darting past the market stalls, the girls followed the evil enchantress out of Hobbleton and on towards Shadowmoon Forest.

CHAPTER FIVE

Miss Raven quickened her pace when she reached the wood, rushing down the forest track with her cloak swirling round her. Darting from tree to tree, Goldie, Red and Snow followed her down the overgrown path.

'Where do you think she's going?' murmured Red.

'Maybe she's trying to trap another fairy,'

Goldie whispered as she used the Shadow Flit move to edge a bit closer.

Miss Raven stopped beside a giant toadstool and delved into her pocket. Goldie peered through the branches. Was she trying to trap a fairy in a jar again or something even worse?

A squirrel leaped down from a tree and scampered over to Snow, chattering eagerly. Snow put a finger to her lips to warn the creature to be quiet. The enchantress peered around, her eyes narrowing. Then she hurried away along the forest track with her cloak flying out behind her again.

Goldie signalled wildly to Snow and Red. 'Come on! We can't lose her now.'

Miss Raven rushed to the riverbank and used some stepping stones to cross the water. Reaching the other side, she peered into a large hollow in the bank. Deep rumbling snores echoed from inside. The girls ducked down behind a bush on the opposite bank and waited.

'Maybe there's a bear inside,' said Red.

'It sounds a lot bigger than a bear,' whispered Snow.

Taking a long pointed stick, Miss Raven thrust it sharply into the hole. The snores broke off with a sudden snort. Then a long growl echoed across the river.

Goldie caught her breath as a warty green face appeared at the entrance to the hole. 'It's a troll!' she whispered.

'Why did she wake it?' hissed Red. 'Why would you EVER wake a sleeping troll?'

Miss Raven jumped back as the creature scrambled out, stretching his enormous tree-like arms. Roaring, the troll thumped his chest and bared his crooked teeth.

The enchantress ducked out of sight as the troll thundered down the riverbank. Stretching out her fingers, she pointed to the bush where the girls were hiding. Lightning crackled from her fingertips, but then fizzled out in mid-air. Miss Raven frowned and rubbed her hands together. Then she pointed her fingers once again . . .

ZAP! The bolt of magic hit the bush and swept it away like a leaf in a storm. With their hiding place gone, the three girls found themselves staring straight into the eyes of a very grumpy troll.

'Uh-oh!' said Red. 'She's set that troll on us.'

'She must have known we were following her!' gasped Goldie.

'We should have put on our ninja clothes,' said Snow, her eyes wide with fright.

 55

The troll let out a huge roar and stomped across the river, spraying water everywhere. Then he thundered up the bank towards them.

'RUN!' yelled Goldie, her heart thumping.

The girls raced away through the trees and the troll thundered after them. Goldie darted through the undergrowth, leaping over fallen logs – hardly daring to look back. 'We can't outrun a troll,' panted Snow.

'Then we'll trip him up!' Red hung back and

stuck out her wooden sword as the troll came closer . . .

The troll stamped on Red's sword with his knobbly foot, snapping it in two. Roaring with laughter, he reached for Red with his big hairy hands.

'Red!' Goldie squealed, pulling her friend out of the way.

'ME GET YOU!' boomed the troll, knocking branches aside and kicking down bushes.

'Now what are we going to do?' cried Snow.

'I've got an idea!' yelled Goldie. 'Just keep him busy.' She stashed her rucksack with Caramel inside by the roots of a tree and began shinning up the tree trunk.

'Hey, troll! I'm over here!' Red jumped up and down, waving at the huge hairy creature.

Still chuckling, the troll swiped at Red and knocked her over. Snow quickly aimed an arrow, which bounced off his nose, leaving him rubbing his face and staring around in confusion. Goldie climbed and climbed until she was high enough to leap from the tree on to the troll's shoulders. Grabbing hold of his huge greasy ears, she clambered up to the top of his head.

'GRRRR, GET OFF!'

yelled the troll, flailing wildly.

Struggling to keep her balance, Goldie began dancing on top of the troll's thick skull. The creature bellowed, trying to shake her off. Then, lowering his head, he rushed straight at a tree trunk . . .

'Watch out, Goldie!' cried Red.

Goldie sprang from the troll's head just before he ran into the tree and knocked himself out. He wobbled for a moment before tumbling to the ground in a daze.

'Troll down!' cheered Red.

'Are you okay?' Snow helped Goldie up.

Goldie brushed the dirt off her skirt and looked around. 'I'm all right, but where's Miss Raven?'

'She used the troll to get rid of us,' Snow said gloomily.

'We'll find her!' Red said, scanning the forest. 'She can't have gone far.'

Groaning, the troll clutched his head. Caramel scrambled out of Goldie's rucksack and sniffed the troll suspiciously.

'This way, Caramel!' Goldie picked up her

bag, and together they all headed back to the empty riverbank.

Goldie spotted a cluster of fairies flitting through the trees. 'Hello, can you help us?' she called. 'We're looking for an enchantress in a grey cloak who came this way.'

'Maybe they can grant us some more wishes too!' Red said eagerly.

The fairies flew down and hovered above the girls' heads.

'What are you doing in our forest?' a blue fairy asked suspiciously.

'That enchantress is a Fairy Catcher!' snapped a green fairy. 'She's a baddie, and if you're her friends then you're baddies too.'

'We're not her friends. We're just trying to find out what she's up to,' Goldie explained quickly.

The green fairy began circling round them, waving her wand. 'She's hunting fairies!' she squealed. 'And maybe you're trying to catch us too.'

'I'm not – I promise!' said Goldie. 'I'm the one who rescued a fairy.'

But the other fairies started circling too, waving their wands faster and faster. Caramel whined and hid behind Goldie's legs as the air filled with glitter from the fairies' wands. Goldie sneezed, sending some of the fairies tumbling into a bush. Red swatted one of them with her broken sword, and at last they all zipped away into the trees.

'I guess they're not going to help us find Miss Raven then,' said Snow.

'Or give us more wishes,' added Red.

Three rabbits hopped out of a nearby burrow.

Snow knelt down to speak to them and then straightened up. 'It's all right! I know where Miss Raven's gone. The animals saw her heading down that track over there.'

'Good work, Snow!' said Red. 'Let's put on our ninja suits, and then she won't spot us this time.'

They changed outfits quickly. Then Goldie lifted Caramel into her backpack again, and they headed into the trees. At last, they caught sight of Miss Raven crouching behind a tree close to a shady pool. A small herd of unicorns stood grazing by the water.

Goldie caught her breath. What was Miss Raven up to this time? Edging closer, the girls watched as the enchantress stretched out her fingers and pointed straight at the unicorns.

CHAPTER SIX

Goldie gazed at Miss Raven in horror. If the enchantress was about to cast another wicked spell, then she had to find a way to warn the poor unicorns. Quickly grabbing a stone, she threw it as hard as she could. Sailing through the air, the pebble landed in the pool with a loud PLOP!

The unicorns lifted their heads in surprise

and whinnied loudly. Then they galloped away into the trees.

Miss Raven looked around suspiciously. Goldie, Red and Snow kept very still, hidden behind the trees in their ninja suits. Wrapping her cloak around her, Miss Raven hurried on down the forest path, stopping at a clearing where magical silver-wing butterflies were resting on a carpet of purple lilies. Goldie, Red and Snow tiptoed after her. Slowly, the enchantress drew a net from her cloak.

'She's trying to catch the forest animals,' muttered Red.

'Not just any animals! She's after the magical ones,' whispered Snow. 'First the fairies and the unicorns, and now the silver-wing butterflies.'

'What does she want them for?' Red hissed. 'It doesn't make any sense.'

Miss Raven edged closer to the butterflies, raising her net.

Snow cupped her hands to her mouth, copying the sound of a falcon. '*Wheo-wheeo!*'

At once, the butterflies spread their wings and fluttered away into the air. Miss Raven swung round again, frowning deeply. After scanning the trees for a long time, she tucked the net under her cloak and continued on her way.

'I think I know what she's doing,' Goldie said slowly. 'She's after the magical animals

66

because she wants to steal their magic.'

'Why would she want their magic?' asked Snow.

'Her own spells aren't working properly,' Goldie explained. 'She was really trying to turn my dad into a troll not a duck.'

Red's eyes widened. 'I'm glad her spell went wrong then!'

'Quick!' Snow nudged the others. 'We're going to lose her.'

They dashed after Miss Raven, who was marching down a slope towards a mass of tall golden trees. Sunlight danced on the bright leaves overhead, and from deep inside the tree trunks the girls heard the whisper of magic. They ducked behind a bush as the enchantress stopped for a moment.

'Where are we?' Snow muttered.

'It's Golden Valley where the forest fairies live,' said Goldie. 'I remember it from Madame Hart's map.'

'Then she's trying to trap fairies again,' said Red. 'We have to warn them. Then we can go back to Hobbleton and use that last *W-I-S-H* to turn your dad back to normal.'

'That's a great plan!' Goldie nodded. 'Hey, where did Miss Raven go?'

They sneaked out of their hiding place, but the enchantress had vanished. A long net, as delicate as a spider's web, was strung between two of the golden trees.

'Looks like she's planning to catch lots of fairies in one go,' said Snow. 'Let's take this net down before they get hurt.'

Goldie tried to cut the net with her sword. 'I can't! It's too strong.'

'Let me try!' Red chopped at it, but the sticky web stuck to the blade.

'Wait here, Caramel!' Goldie set the bear cub down by a tree and began clambering up the trunk. Struggling with the knot, she tried to untie the net from the branches.

'Let's do this together!' Red called from below. 'You stay there, Goldie, and Snow can climb up that tree on the other side.' She waited while Snow clambered up. 'Ready? One, two, three – PULL!'

Goldie and Snow tugged at the net from opposite ends, while Red yanked on the middle. The net stretched wider and wider. Then suddenly the whole thing unravelled and fell down, dragging Snow and Goldie with it. The girls all tumbled to the ground, tangled up in the sticky web.

'Well, well!' said a sharp voice. 'It looks like I've caught three annoying little girls.' Miss Raven crept out from behind a tree like a spider. Her eyes flashed as she stood over them. 'Did you really think you could defeat me with no skills, no magic and very little brainpower?'

Goldie's heart sank, but she wasn't going to show the enchantress that she was scared. 'We have more brainpower than you!' she said bravely.

Miss Raven smiled thinly. 'It doesn't look that way. You're trapped, so I've won! Soon I'll have all the magic I need to be the most powerful enchantress in the kingdom.'

'But your magic isn't working properly, is it?' said Red. 'That's why you're trying to steal magic from other creatures.'

Miss Raven scowled. 'I have enough power to cast a spell on you, child! Maybe Hobbleton should have three more ducks. Let's see!' She stretched out her fingers.

Caramel squeaked and hid under a pile of leaves. Goldie's heart thumped. She REALLY didn't want to be turned into a duck.

'No way! You're not getting us with your stupid spell!' Red tried to swing her sword, but it was tangled in the sticky web.

'Stop it, Red!' said Goldie. 'You're making things worse.'

'We've got to do something!' panted Red.

The enchantress smiled nastily and pointed at the three girls. Goldie waited for the flash of magic from her fingertips, but nothing happened. Miss Raven grimaced and flexed her fingers. Then she pointed at the girls again, but still nothing happened.

'Frogspawn!' she muttered. 'Why isn't it working?'

 71

She stretched her hands out again. Suddenly a flash of lightning burst from her fingers and struck a bush, melting it into a puddle of frogspawn.

'Ugh!' groaned Miss Raven. 'I didn't mean turn *into* frogspawn!'

Panicking, Goldie struggled with the sticky net. Ending up as a duck would be bad, but becoming frogspawn would be a lot worse!

'We need to get out of here!' she cried.

'I KNOW!' snapped Red, still wrestling with the net.

Caramel climbed out of her hiding place and scampered towards them. Goldie tried to signal to the little bear cub to stay back. She didn't want Caramel getting trapped too.

The enchantress lifted her arms again.

'I can make this spell work! *Give me magic, give me luck and turn these girls into a duck!*'

Just as the lightning zapped from Miss Raven's fingertips, Caramel leaped forward and bit her on the ankle. The enchantress squealed, stumbling sideways. Her spell burst up into the air and blew the leaves off the nearest tree. The golden leaves tumbled down, each one transforming into a fluffy yellow duckling as it fell. Landing on the soft earth, the ducklings scurried into the undergrowth, cheeping loudly.

'BLAST!' shrieked Miss Raven. 'Look what you've done, you stupid bear! I'll turn you into a toad. I'll make you into a mouse!'

'Run, Caramel!' shouted Goldie.

Caramel scrambled into a bush as Miss Raven took aim at her. Lightning zapped from the enchantress's fingers, rebounding off a tree trunk and hitting her grey cloak. The cloak rippled and shimmered. Then it transformed into hundreds of little mice all running up and down her arms. Miss Raven flapped wildly as she tried to shake them off.

Red giggled. 'She turned her own cloak into mice!'

'Stop laughing!' yelled Miss Raven. 'I'll turn everyone in your ridiculous town into a duck – you'll see! There'll be nobody left by the time I'm finished.' And she rushed away through the trees, still shaking mice off her arms.

'Caramel, you saved us!' said Snow.

The bear cub scrambled out of her hiding place, squeaking happily.

'You're such a clever bear!' Goldie told her fondly. 'Quick – let's get out of here! We have to get back to help my dad and stop Miss Raven changing the whole of Hobbleton into ducks.'

CHAPTER SEVEN

Goldie, Red and Snow spent a very long time trying to wriggle free from the net or cut it with their swords. The sticky web stuck to their hair and their clothes. They stopped for a little while to eat the chocolate cake and cheese-and-pickle sandwiches from their rucksacks, but the web stuck to those too.

Soon the sun disappeared behind the trees

and the forest grew dark.
The fluffy yellow ducklings
huddled up next to Caramel
and went to sleep.

Goldie glanced at the moonlit sky. 'What are
we going to do? Everyone in Hobbleton could be
a duck by now.'

Red tried hacking at the web again with her
broken sword. 'I – want – to – be – free!'

'This isn't working,' said Snow.

'You hold the net, and Red and I will try to cut
it,' said Goldie, lifting her sword.

Together they chopped and sliced at the net
as hard as they could, but the silky web still
wouldn't break.

'It must be enchanted,' said Red. 'We'll have to
find a different way out. Who's got a good idea?'

They all fell silent. A cold wind ruffled the

trees, and an owl hooted somewhere in the distance. Goldie rubbed her forehead. Her stomach was rumbling and she was starting to get a headache. 'This is stupid!' she cried. 'I wish this net would just go away!'

Her words echoed round the forest. There was a flash of purple light and the net vanished completely. Goldie gasped, and then a terrible icy feeling sank all the way to her boots.

'Oh, Goldie!' said Red. 'You've used up the second W-I-S-H. Now we've only got half of one left.'

Goldie swallowed, tears pricking her eyes. 'I didn't mean to! I just wasn't thinking.'

'I'm always doing that,' said Red.

'We'll have to find a way to make the half one work,' said Snow. 'We'd better change out of these ninja clothes and get back to Hobbleton.'

Goldie picked up Caramel and followed the others down the forest path. Her head was thumping. How could she have been so silly, using up their last full wish like that? She had really needed it to turn her dad back to normal.

Daylight began to creep into the sky as they reached Hobbleton. The clock on the town hall chimed six o'clock. The streets were empty, and everyone seemed to be asleep, except for a duck with a yellow beak swimming round and round the pond.

'That duck looks like your dad in a funny sort of way,' said Snow. 'I thought you left him in the bath?'

'He must have found his way out.' Goldie crouched beside the pond. 'Dad, is that you? Are you all right?'

The duck quacked and waggled his tail feathers cheerfully.

Goldie took a deep breath. She would use the half a wish to try and break the spell on her dad. 'I WISH the duck spell was broken.' She stared hopefully at the duck, waiting for a flash of purple light, but nothing happened.

'I WISH my dad was normal again!' she said firmly.

The duck dipped his beak in the water and nibbled some pondweed.

'I WISH this duck spell would go away!' Goldie wailed. 'It isn't working. You can't do ANYTHING with half a wish!'

Snow put an arm round Goldie's shoulders, steering her away from the pond. 'We'll figure something out. There's still a way to break the enchantment – I'm sure of it.'

'I'll be back soon!' Goldie called to her dad. 'And I'll save you from that spell – I promise.'

The girls hurried across the empty market square to the Three Spoons Hotel. A cart came rumbling through the streets, and the smell of fresh bread drifted out of the bakery.

'No one else seems to have turned into a duck,' Red pointed out. 'So maybe Miss Raven hasn't come back yet.'

'There's only one way to find out.' Goldie hurried inside. Leaving a very sleepy Caramel in the kitchen, she headed upstairs to Miss Raven's room. Taking a deep breath, she slowly opened the door . . . to find the room was empty. Miss

Raven's magic book, *How to Make Your Spells Sparkle*, still lay on the chest of drawers next to the potion bottles.

'I'm glad she's not here!' Snow looked round with wide eyes.

'That just means she's out somewhere trying to trap a unicorn or a fairy, and steal their magic,' Red said gloomily.

'And that means her powers aren't strong enough yet,' said Goldie. 'So maybe we could use her own magic to beat her?'

'Don't be silly! We can't do spells,' scoffed Red.

Goldie picked up the spellbook and leafed through the pages. 'A few months back, we'd never done sword-fighting or ninja moves either! You're not scared of trying something new, are you?'

'No!' Red said huffily. 'I just don't want to turn myself into a frog.'

 83

Goldie's eyes flashed. 'Don't you see? This is our chance to protect everyone in Hobbleton . . . and once we've beaten Miss Raven she'll HAVE to turn my dad back to normal again.'

'All right then!' Red peered at the book. 'Here's a good one – turn your enemy into strawberry yoghurt. Or how about this? Make your foe sneeze for a hundred years!'

'I love both those spells!' Goldie's eyes lit up.

'But Miss Raven won't be able to reverse the duck spell if she's turned into strawberry yoghurt,' Snow pointed out. 'Anyway, how are you going to make that magical lightning shoot out of your fingers?'

Goldie frowned. Snow had a good point.

'How about a potion? We could make one of those.' Snow took the spellbook and flicked through it until she found the right chapter.

'Yes – potions!' Goldie leaned over to study the book. 'Potions that turn you purple, potions that make you wiser ... Wait – this one's perfect!' She pointed at the page.

'A shrinking potion!' said Red. 'Great idea! Miss Raven won't be half as scary if she's the size of a mouse.'

'Gather moonweed and stinging nettles,' Snow read out. 'Chop them up and mix them with toad spit and the breath of an ice dragon. Then heat the mixture till it bubbles. Add crumbs from a gingerbread man and stir everything carefully.'

'Then, if we're lucky, we can add it to Miss Raven's breakfast,' said Goldie.

'I can get the ice-dragon's breath,' said Snow.

'I'll fetch the gingerbread man and the nettles and moonweed,' Red said quickly.

 85

'Okay, I'll get the toad spit then!' Goldie snapped the spellbook shut. 'Let's meet back here in half an hour. Then we'll magic up the perfect potion!'

CHAPTER EIGHT

Grabbing a dish from the kitchen, Goldie dashed outside and searched for a toad in the reeds that grew beside the pond. The sun was climbing higher in the sky, and she needed to get the toad spit before the streets filled with people.

The first toad she found dived into the water, and the second one refused to open its mouth. Goldie hunted round the muddy bank until

87

at last she found another toad – the largest, slimiest one she'd ever seen. Grimacing, she gathered some dribble from around its mouth. On the opposite bank, she could see her dad swimming around and nibbling pondweed. Her heart thumped quickly. This potion plan really had to work! She wanted her dad back again.

Hurrying back into the hotel kitchen, she took the huge copper saucepan down from the shelf and added more wood to the fire. 'It's time to make a potion!' she told Caramel, who was still snoozing on the rug.

Her mum came in, yawning. 'Morning, Goldie! Thank you for getting up so early and starting the porridge. The guests will be very happy.'

'Er . . . that's okay!' Goldie quickly hid the dish of toad spit as her mum came over to hug her.

'Have you seen your dad?' her mum went on.

'I think he went out for firewood, but he didn't return last night, and I'm getting a bit worried.'

'I saw him a little while ago,' Goldie said truthfully.

'That's good.' Her mum smiled. 'I'll lay the breakfast tables for the guests. You carry on with that porridge!'

As soon as her mum left, Red and Snow ran inside.

'I've got the nettles, the moonweed and the gingerbread man!' shouted Red.

'*Shh!*' Goldie scowled. 'My mum thinks I'm cooking porridge for everyone's breakfast.'

Snow giggled. 'Nettles and toad spit! Delicious!'

Goldie chopped the moonweed and stinging nettles and threw them in the copper pan. Then she added the toad spit and tipped up the misty jar of ice-dragon's breath that Snow had

gathered. Heating the mixture on the stove, she added some crumbs from the gingerbread.

'It's a waste of a gingerbread man,' Red grumbled.

The potion turned brown and then bright red, and the smell of stinky socks filled the kitchen. Red coughed and opened a window. At last, the mixture turned a glowing yellow, like magical overripe bananas, and bubbled gently in the bottom of the pan.

'How's the porridge coming along, Goldie?' her mum called down the corridor.

'Er . . . it's good!' Goldie called back. Then she nudged Snow and whispered, 'Pass me that bag of oats – quick!'

Fetching a new saucepan, Goldie added oats and milk and mixed up some porridge at top speed. She added raisins and blueberries and a very large helping of honey.

The front door banged, and footsteps rang out on the tiled floor.

'Why isn't my breakfast ready?' said a sharp voice. 'I'm *extremely* hungry, and I don't expect to be kept waiting!'

Goldie, Snow and Red froze.

'That's Miss Raven!' hissed Red. 'This is perfect! We can slip the potion into her breakfast. Is it ready yet?'

'It's ready!' Goldie gave the bright yellow mixture one more stir.

'Don't worry, breakfast is almost ready,' they heard Goldie's mum say to Miss Raven. 'Why don't you come and sit down? I'll take that bag if you like—'

'Don't touch that!' snapped the enchantress.

 92

'You must never touch my things.'

'As you wish,' Mrs Locks said calmly. 'Would you like to come this way?'

Goldie peeked round the door and saw Miss Raven disappearing into the dining room, clutching a bulging sack. 'She's definitely caught some magical creature,' she told the others.

'Poor thing!' whispered Snow.

'She's changed her cloak back to normal too,' said Red. 'Quick, your mum's coming!'

Goldie hid the potion under a tea towel just as her mum rushed back into the kitchen.

'Hello, girls!' She looked surprised to see Red and Snow. 'Have you both come for breakfast? I think everyone in Hobbleton wants to try Goldie's famous porridge!'

'Mmm, smells delicious!' said Red, using a saucepan lid to fan away the smell of stinky socks.

 93

'We're just here to help Goldie,' added Snow. 'We won't get in the way.'

Goldie's head whirled. She had to add the potion to Miss Raven's porridge, but she couldn't do it with her mum watching. 'Why don't I dish up the porridge and—'

'I'll just take the whole saucepan. Some of the guests are very hungry.' Mrs Locks grabbed the porridge pan and some bowls, and headed back to the dining room.

'Now what do we do?' hissed Red. 'We need to put the potion in Miss Raven's breakfast.'

Goldie grabbed a new saucepan. 'If she's hungry, she'll want a second helping!'

Stirring quickly, she cooked more porridge and spooned it into a row of bowls. Then she poured the glowing yellow potion into one dish and mixed it into the porridge as fast as she could.

Snow grabbed a maid's cap and apron from the kitchen cupboard. 'Wear this! If Miss Raven recognises you, she's sure to be suspicious.'

Goldie tucked her golden hair under the cap and pulled it down over her forehead. Then, taking a deep breath, she rushed down the corridor with the tray full of porridge.

CHAPTER NINE

Goldie kept her head down as she sneaked into the hotel dining room. Remembering her ninja training, she used a Swan Glide move to slip inside and set down the porridge tray without a sound. She couldn't let Miss Raven see her.

The room had filled up with guests, and Mrs Locks was pouring orange juice and filling up the teapot. Goldie picked up the porridge bowl with the potion inside and crept towards the dining table. Miss Raven was sitting with her back to the door, gobbling down her breakfast. The bulging sack lay at her feet, and something was wriggling inside.

'Second helpings, anyone?' Goldie's mum came bustling over.

'Yes, please!' said a gentleman in a velvet jacket. 'This is delicious! You must give me the recipe.'

Mrs Locks held out her hand for Goldie's porridge bowl. 'Thank you, honey. I'll take that.'

Goldie's heart raced. She couldn't let someone else eat the potion! She quickly grabbed a second bowl from the tray and passed it over. Her mum gave her a puzzled look as she handed it to the gentleman.

 97

'Where's MY second helping?' Miss Raven banged her spoon down on the table.

Goldie quickly glided over and, without a word, she set the porridge with the potion down in front of the enchantress. Then she tiptoed away and ducked behind a curtain.

'Oh! Who put that there?' Miss Raven looked around suspiciously. 'And why does it look so yellow?'

'It's the extra honey, I should think,' said Mrs Locks, filling up her teacup.

Goldie watched, holding her breath. Miss Raven stared at the yellowish porridge. Then at last she scooped some on to her spoon and lifted it to her mouth.

Suddenly a loud squawking came from the sack at her feet.

Miss Raven slammed down her spoon again.

 98

'Be quiet, you!' she yelled, aiming a kick at the bag, but the creature inside squirmed and chirped even louder.

Mrs Locks put down her teapot. 'Miss Raven, I hope you haven't trapped some poor animal in there?'

'None of your business!' the enchantress replied, reaching for the sack just as a sharp yellow beak pecked through the cloth and two amber eyes peeped out.

A baby firebird wriggled out of the bag and fluttered on to the breakfast table, knocking over the orange juice. Flames flickered across its golden wings. The hotel guests gasped and the gentleman in the velvet jacket turned pale with fright.

'Come back here!' Miss Raven grabbed the firebird's neck, and Goldie jumped out of her

 99

hiding place before she could stop herself.

'Leave that creature alone!' she yelled.

The enchantress let go of the firebird in surprise just as Red and Snow dashed into the room. The firebird flapped quickly out of reach.

Miss Raven's eyes narrowed. 'You three again! Why do I get the feeling you've been up to more mischief?'

'Goldie, what's going on?' said Mrs Locks.

'She's an enchantress!' cried Goldie. 'And

you're all in terrible danger!'

Miss Raven muttered a spell to herself, and lightning began to crackle at her fingertips. The guests started running for the door.

Goldie turned to Red and Snow, whispering, 'You distract her! I'll go for the porridge.'

Red nodded. 'Hey, Miss Raven! Why are your spells so terrible?' she called out.

'Why can't you make your magic work?' added Snow.

'How dare you! I'll show you how well my magic works!' shrieked the enchantress, stretching out her fingers.

Goldie darted round the escaping guests and sprang up on to the table. Dodging a lightning bolt from Miss Raven's fingertips, she snatched up the enchantress's bowl. Scooping some porridge on to a spoon, she flicked it straight at Miss Raven's face. The blob of porridge soared through the air and hit the enchantress right in the mouth. Miss Raven swallowed it down with a look of surprise.

Goldie waited, her heart pounding.

'Ugh!' cried the enchantress. 'That's horrible! And everyone thinks your porridge is so wonderful. Well, I think it's absolutely revolting!' Goldie stuck

her hands on her hips. 'That's not my usual porridge.'

Miss Raven clutched her throat. 'What do you mean? What did you put in my bowl?'

'Moonweed, nettles and toad spit,' Red told her.

'Toad spit?' Miss Raven shrieked, her eyes wide with shock.

Suddenly a whistling noise filled the room – like air escaping from a pricked balloon. The enchantress stretched out her fingers . . . but they began to shrink like tiny sausages. Then her hands and arms shrank too. Her legs grew shorter and shorter, as if they were melting. Her long grey cloak dropped to the floor, and her little body almost disappeared inside it. She went on shrinking till she was smaller than a pumpkin . . . smaller than a cabbage . . . smaller than a teacup!

The firebird fluttered over to gaze at the tiny enchantress. Then it squawked and pecked at her crossly. Miss Raven gave a squeak and hid inside the folds of her enormous cloak.

'We did it!' yelled Red. 'We finally beat her!'

Goldie scrambled down from the table and scooped Miss Raven into an empty porridge bowl. The enchantress shook her tiny fist and shouted squeakily.

'Goldie, what are you doing?' cried her mum. 'I really don't understand.'

'I'll explain everything soon, I promise,' said Goldie. 'But there's something I've got to do first.'

Carrying the teeny-tiny enchantress in the bowl, she rushed out into the town square, followed by Snow and Red. Dashing over to the pond, she found her dad paddling around by the reeds. He flapped his wings and quacked loudly as soon as he saw Goldie.

'Turn my dad back to normal!' Goldie told Miss Raven firmly.

'Never!' squeaked the enchantress. 'He looks much better as a duck.'

'Change him back,' Goldie snapped, 'or we won't help you get back to your normal size again.'

Miss Raven sighed and tapped her tiny foot. 'I suppose I could reverse my spell . . . although you really don't deserve it!'

Goldie waited for crackling magic to pour out of the enchantress's fingertips, but instead a buzzing noise filled the air. A cluster of fairies came fluttering over the rooftops. They soared over the market square, heading straight for Goldie.

'There she is!' shrieked a purple fairy. 'She's the one that was trying to hurt us.'

'Get her!' squealed another. 'She has to pay for what she's done!'

Goldie stepped back in alarm. 'It wasn't me, I promise! I've never tried to trap a fairy.'

'No, not you! We want HER!' The purple fairy pointed to Miss Raven.

Goldie suddenly recognised her as the fairy she'd rescued from the glass jar the day before.

Swooping down from the sky, the horde of fairies seized hold of Miss Raven's tiny arms and legs. With a burst of glittery fairy dust, they swept her up into the air, whooping in triumph.

107

'Put me down!' howled Miss Raven. 'How dare you treat me this way?'

But the fairies ignored her. Cheering and clapping, they spun round and zipped away across the rooftops again.

'Come back!' shouted Goldie. 'I just need her to cast one more spell.'

But the fairies sped off into the sky, carrying the enchantress with them.

'What am I going to do now?' cried Goldie.

Snow put a hand on her arm. 'There's still that half a wish. I know it didn't work last time, but I think you should give it one more try.'

CHAPTER TEN

Goldie stared doubtfully at her dad on the other side of the pond. He was still swimming around and dabbling his beak in the water. 'I don't think it will make any difference. Half-wishes don't come true!'

Two more ducks flew overhead and landed in the water, and Goldie's dad paddled towards them, quacking loudly.

'What about the spellbook? There must be something in there,' said Red.

Goldie shook her head. 'I've already looked, and I couldn't find anything that'll help.'

Red studied the ducks and frowned. 'He looks quite happy . . . Maybe he's got used to being a duck, and that makes it hard to switch back again.'

'Red, that's brilliant!' cried Snow. 'We could find things that remind him of being human – that might make a difference.'

A tiny flame of hope lit up in Goldie's chest. 'That could really work! And I think I know what will help him.' She ran back to the hotel and rushed upstairs to her parents' bedroom.

Gathering up her dad's slippers and the checked cap he always wore, she raced back downstairs again. Red and Snow were waiting for her in the kitchen.

'Slippers and cap,' Snow noted. 'What else? Think really hard!'

Goldie's mind whirled. What would remind her dad of the person he used to be? She spotted a blue plate with some leftover cherry cake. Her dad had eaten the last slice the day before and only a few crumbs remained, but it was his favourite so maybe that would be enough! Grabbing the plate, she dashed outside.

Her dad was swimming round and round the pond with the other two ducks.

'Dad?' Goldie called hopefully, but he took no notice so she called again.

At last, her dad paddled over and stopped at the water's edge. Goldie threw some crumbs of cherry cake on to the bank. 'Here, Dad! Remember this? It's your favourite.'

 111

Her dad hopped out of the water and pecked at the cake crumbs. Then he tilted his head to one side and gazed at Goldie curiously. Goldie tiptoed closer and knelt down beside him.

'And these are your slippers and cap.' She laid his things down on the bank.

Her dad pecked the cap and looked at her again.

'You do remember, don't you? This is who you are! You're not a duck at all,' she told him. 'You like cherry cake and cups of tea, and you always whistle a tune when you're working in the kitchen.'

Her dad fluffed his tail feathers and listened with his head on one side.

'Keep going!' urged Snow. 'What did he like to whistle?'

Goldie began whistling the tune to 'Dance in

the Stormy Weather', her dad's favourite song, and he flapped his wings and quacked as if he was joining in.

Goldie broke off with a tear in her eye. 'I love you, Dad!' she said. 'You will come back to me, won't you?'

'Quack, QUACK!' said Goldie's dad, and he pecked at his slippers urgently.

'I think it's all coming back to him!' said Red.

'Quick, say the wish!' Snow cried.

Goldie drew a huge breath. 'I WISH my dad was back to normal again!'

There was a flash of purple light. Goldie's dad stretched his wings and waggled his tail feathers. Then a gust of wind blew in, lifting him into the sky and spinning him round. Sparkly magic filled the air like stardust, and Goldie had to shade her eyes from the dazzling brightness.

Her dad's legs grew longer and straighter, and his webbed feet disappeared. Then, very slowly, his feathery wings transformed into arms. He grew taller and taller until he towered over them with a huge smile on his face. The people setting up their market stalls in the town square looked over and shook their heads.

'Are you feeling okay, Mr Locks?' said Red.

Mr Locks stared at his arms and legs. Then he flapped his elbows, looking very puzzled.

'Dad, are you all right?' Goldie asked anxiously.

'I think so!' said her dad. 'But I had this really strange dream about being a duck.' He picked up his cap and stuck it on his head.

Goldie took his arm. 'Yes, it was very strange. It's probably best if you don't think about it. Shall we go inside and get a cup of tea?'

Her dad frowned. 'Are you telling me I actually WAS a duck?'

'Well, there was a wicked enchantress called Miss Raven,' explained Red. 'It's quite a funny tale actually.'

Goldie's mum appeared at the front door of the hotel with a firebird in her arms. 'I caught this creature at last, but what are we going to do with it?'

Suddenly dozens of people rushed across the town square wanting to look at the firebird and ask about the fairies. The hotel guests ventured nervously outside to see if Miss Raven had really disappeared. They all congratulated Goldie's mum and dad on defeating the evil enchantress.

'Well, I'm not quite sure how we did it!' said Goldie's dad, scratching his head. 'I think it was just good luck.'

'Good luck and porridge!' Mrs Locks added with a wink.

'They don't even know that it was us who beat her!' huffed Red.

Snow pulled Red away from the crowd. 'Shh, we can't tell anyone! If they find out what we've been up to, then we'll never get to go on more adventures.'

'Snow's right! They'll say it's too dangerous,' Goldie agreed.

Mrs Locks hurried over and put the little firebird into Goldie's arms. 'I don't know where Miss Raven snatched this poor creature from, but I'm sure that you three

are the best people to get it home again. Try to be back by dinnertime!'

She gave them a hug and a wave.

Goldie gazed down at the little golden bird. 'His home could be miles away! It might take us days to find it.'

'Not if we fly!' Red's eyes lit up. 'It's time to fetch the flying carpet!'

CHAPTER ELEVEN

Goldie, Red and Snow hurried into the empty dance studio at the Glass Slipper Academy and searched the secret storeroom behind the mirror. The flying carpet was curled up behind a rack of ninja costumes, dozing gently. When Goldie called to it, the rug stretched out and shook its tassels. A dark patch at one end showed where it had once been scorched by a dragon's breath.

'Hey, rug!' Red said loudly. 'We need a ride.'

The rug flew to the darkest corner of the storeroom and rolled itself up very tightly.

'You scared it!' sighed Goldie.

'Let me try!' Snow crawled into the corner and gently stroked the rug's tassels. 'How would you like to go on an adventure?' she whispered. 'Do you remember how wonderful it felt zooming up into the air and soaring across Waybeyond?'

The rug unrolled a tiny bit and jiggled its tassels.

'Come with us and you can fly like that again!' said Snow, and, with a lot of coaxing, she got the rug to follow her into the dance studio.

Goldie held the carpet still while everyone climbed on. Then she clambered on last and held the baby firebird in her lap. 'Right then, carpet!'

she said cheerfully. 'We're looking for this little firebird's home. So don't go too fast—'

Her words were whipped away as the carpet burst out of the dance academy like a speeding arrow. It whizzed up into the air and spun round three times, before zipping away over the rooftops.

'I said don't go too fast!' yelled Goldie.

Snow stroked the carpet, and eventually it slowed down a little so that they could see where they were going. They headed south-west over rolling hills and meadows until they reached Redrock Canyon, where many of the firebirds lived.

Goldie peered down at the dusty red valley. Firebird nests lined the cliffs and a sand dragon was lazing in the sun. 'Is this your home?' she asked the firebird.

The creature squawked and shook its head.

'We'd better try somewhere else,' said Red.

'Let's head north a bit.'

The carpet whirled round and zoomed off again. At last they reached the Rippling River and the firebird's eyes suddenly lit up as they sailed over a sandy cliff near the riverbank.

Flapping its fiery wings, it gave a loud cry.

'Down, carpet!' cried Goldie, and the rug plunged through the sky so fast they almost tumbled off.

Landing on the riverbank, the carpet stretched out its tassels and settled down for a rest. A flock of firebirds flew down to greet the baby bird, who hopped along the bank and cheeped happily.

Goldie smiled as she watched them touch beaks and preen their wings.

'That's another mission completed!' Red declared, dusting off her hands.

'And another baddie defeated!' added Goldie.

'I suppose we ought to get back to Hobbleton,' said Snow. 'I've got loads of shirts to sew, and your mum will want help in the shop, Red.'

'And the guests will want more porridge soon!' sighed Goldie. 'I should probably get cooking right away . . .'

The girls frowned as they gazed at the river. The firebirds began to swoop over the water. A mermaid was teaching some frogs to dance on the opposite bank. Breaking through the surface, a herd of river horses shook sparkly drops of water off their manes. One with a silver-grey coat looked over at the girls and gave a loud whinny.

'I think she's asking if we want to go for a ride!' Snow said excitedly.

Goldie ran down to the water's edge with her friends following. More river horses swam over, splashing and neighing. Their horse bodies narrowed into powerful mermaid tails that they used for diving through the water.

Goldie's heart began to race. She'd ridden a unicorn before, but never a river horse. 'They'll just have to find someone else to cook the porridge!' she said quickly.

'Yes, and do the sewing!' cried Snow.

'Well, what are we waiting for?' Red clambered on to a golden river horse.

Goldie waded into the shallows and climbed on to the silver-grey horse, holding tight to the creature's mane. The horses began to leap and dive across the river. Water whooshed round them, and glittering drops flew high into the air. Goldie beamed, her curly hair flying out behind her. She loved going on new adventures in Waybeyond!